A note to the reader:

Always exercise caution when engaging in any activities that involve food preparation or cooking.
Children should always be under adult supervision, especially around hot ovens and stoves, blenders,
mixers, knives, and other sharp instruments. Be mindful of food allergies before preparing any recipe.
Brand name ingredients mentioned in this cookbook are trademarks of their respective companies,
which are not associated in any way with this publication. The mention of such ingredients is for
reference purposes only and does not constitute or imply an endorsement or recommendation by
the publisher.

CE

Copyright © 2006 Sesame Workshop.
Sesame Street Muppets copyright © 2006 Sesame Workshop.
All rights reserved under International and
Pan-American Copyright Conventions.
"Sesame Street®", "Sesame Workshop", and their logos are
trademarks and service marks of Sesame Workshop.
Published by Reader's Digest Children's Books
Reader's Digest Road, Pleasantville, NY U.S.A. 10570-7000
and Reader's Digest Children's Publishing Limited,
The Ice House, 124-126 Walcot Street, Bath UK BA1 5BG
Reader's Digest Children's Books is a trademark and
Reader's Digest is a registered trademark of
The Reader's Digest Association, Inc. Manufactured in China.
10 9 8 7 6 5 4 3 2 1

Big Block Party!

written by Deborah November
illustrated by Joe Mathieu

Reader's Digest Children's Books™

Pleasantville, New York • Montréal, Québec • Bath, United Kingdom

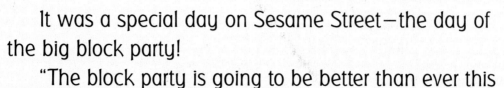

It was a special day on Sesame Street—the day of the big block party!

"The block party is going to be better than ever this year!" said Zoe. "I can't wait to see what special foods everyone brings! Elmo, what are *you* bringing to the block party?" she asked.

Big Block
Party

"Elmo's not sure yet," Elmo replied.
"Well you'd better make up your mind!"
Zoe laughed. "The party starts soon!"

Elmo followed Zoe into Hooper's Store.

"I have to buy all the ingredients for my special recipe," Zoe explained to Elmo.

It looked like all of Sesame Street was in Hooper's Store buying ingredients. Hooper's Store was hopping!

Elmo looked around trying to decide what he could make for the block party. "What can Elmo make that would be really special?" he wondered.

Elmo decided to go to Zoe's house to help with her recipe.
"Maybe this will give Elmo some ideas," Elmo said.

"I'm going to make my favorite banana-strawberry smoothies," Zoe told Elmo.

"Why are they your favorite?" Elmo wanted to know.

"Because they are the exact same color as my tutu!" Zoe replied.

When they were finished, Elmo tasted some of the leftover smoothie. "Mmmm! Elmo thinks Zoe's Tutu Pink Smoothies are too, too delicious!"

Elmo still didn't know what he wanted to bring to the block party, so he zoomed off to see what Big Bird was making.

"Hi, Big Bird," said Elmo when he got to Big Bird's nest. "What are you making?"

"I'm making Granny Bird's favorite Peanut Butter Eggs to share with everybody. My granny learned how to make them from *her* granny! They remind her of when Big Bird was just a little egg. Want to help roll them?"

"Elmo would love to help," beamed Elmo.

GRAHAM CRACKERS

Non-Fat DRY MILK POWDER

HONEY

PEANUT BUTTER

Wheat Germ

Huff, puff, puff. A very tired Grover was dragging two huge bags of groceries down the street.

"Elmo will help you, Grover!" cried Elmo, as he took one of the bags.

"I, Grover, would appreciate your help," said Grover. "I am making ABC Sandwiches, but 26 letters are very heavy."

Before long, Elmo and Grover were busy making ABC Sandwiches. Grover showed Elmo how to put apple and cheese slices on some bread. "A is for apple. B is for bread. And C is for cheese," explained Grover.

Apple

Bread

Cheese

When they finished, Elmo peeked inside one of the bags and had a great idea.

"Elmo wants to make an ELMO sandwich! Elmo will use an egg for E, lettuce for L, mayonnaise for M, and olives for O."

"That is a scrumptious idea, Elmo," said Grover.

Eggs

Lettuce

Mayonnaise

Olives

Mayonnaise

Elmo still didn't know what to make for the block party. *Maybe Bert and Ernie will help Elmo decide what to bring,* he thought.

Ernie and Bert's kitchen counter looked like a celery stick forest! "Elmo has never seen so much celery before," Elmo giggled.

"Bert and I both decided to make recipes using celery, since celery is one of the foods we both love," Ernie explained.

Cream Cheese

"But our recipes are very different, just like us!" Bert added.

Ernie explained that he was making Tasty Twiddlebug Logs in honor of his favorite little friends, the Twiddlebugs.

"And I am making celery boats in honor of...celery and boats," Bert joked.

Elmo's tummy was beginning to grumble. He was thinking of all the yummy snacks he'd helped his friends make. Then he noticed a wonderful smell wafting around the corner.

Elmo knows where that delicious smell is coming from, thought Elmo. Elmo followed his nose around the corner and...

…sure enough, there was Cookie Monster up to his googly eyes in English muffins, tomatoes, olives, and lots of other delicious stuff.

"Mmm, something smells great," said Elmo. "But where are the cookies?"

"Me make Monster Muffin Pizzas! Pizzas look like cookie, shaped like cookie, but healthier food for monsters than cookie!" declared Cookie Monster.

Elmo helped Cookie Monster make his pizzas and even created a special one all his own.

Elmo left Cookie's place and was walking down the street when he spotted Rosita. "¡*Hola*, Rosita!" said Elmo. "What is in your bag?"

"¡*Hola*, Elmo!" answered Rosita. "I have just returned from the bodega where I bought tortillas!"

"Elmo does not understand," said Elmo.

"A bodega is a grocery store and tortillas are a type of flat Mexican bread," said Rosita. "I am making Cream Cheese Salsa Pinwheels for the block party. They are a special snack because I love salsa!"

"That sounds very tasty, Rosita," said Elmo. "Can you help Elmo think of something special to bring to the block party?"

"Just think about something that is special to you!" said Rosita. "I have to go home and cook now, Elmo. *¡Hasta la vista!*"

As he skipped around the corner, Elmo bumped into Oscar's trash can.

"SCRAM!" hollered Oscar the Grouch. "Slimey and I are creating Delicious Cups of Dirt and making a magnificent mess doing it. Say, what are you bringing to the party, Elmo?"

"Elmo doesn't know," Elmo replied sadly. "Elmo has been all over Sesame Street today, and everyone is preparing special snacks to share. Everyone has great ideas except Elmo."

"I couldn't think of anything either," said Oscar. "But then Slimey had the super grouchy idea for the Delicious Cups of Dirt." If Oscar's special pet worm could come up with such a great idea, Elmo wondered if *his* special pet might have an idea....

Elmo charged into his house. "MOMMMYYY!"
She was in the kitchen feeding Elmo's goldfish, Dorothy.
"Mommy, Elmo has to make something special and delicious for the block party!" cried Elmo. "And it's almost time for it to start!"

Elmo looked at Dorothy and just like that, *Elmo had an idea!*
There was a special snack that Elmo munched on every day after
preschool. It was special to Elmo because it reminded him of his
favorite pet goldfish. Elmo knew it would be the perfect snack to
share with all his friends.

Elmo and Mommy finished up and got to the block party just as it was getting started. All the Sesame Street friends were excited to share their favorite special snacks. Elmo couldn't wait to try all the yummy food...and to share his Favorite Goldfish Snack Mix with all his favorite friends!

"Elmo, I see you thought of something special and delicious to bring," said Zoe, as she crunched on Elmo's snack mix.

"A little fish whispered an idea in Elmo's ear," Elmo giggled.

Cooking with Kids!

Did you know that when children prepare—or help to prepare foods—they are more likely to eat them? That includes foods kids might not be so crazy about, like vegetables and high-fiber "good for you" foods. Kids like to create and have fun, so what could be better than making a snack or meal they can eat *and* share with family and friends?

Cooking with your child is a great way to spend time together and a great way to get even the pickiest eater to eat. It's also a good way to:

◆ introduce new vocabulary words (whisk, garnish, ingredients, etc.)

◆ illustrate simple math concepts (counting teaspoons of an ingredient or cutting things into halves or quarters, making patterns)

◆ help them learn how to follow directions

◆ foster feelings of self-confidence and independence

◆ encourage cooperation and teamwork

What kinds of things can you do to make cooking exciting, engaging, and fun?

◆ Buy a set of measuring spoons, a spatula, and a bowl that is only the child's to use. Keep them in a special place. He'll love having his own cooking supplies just like Mom's or Dad's.

◆ Take children shopping for the ingredients used in the recipe. Let them help choose the pieces of fruit and vegetables.

◆ Younger children can help with safe, simple tasks like washing fruit and vegetables, pouring ingredients into a bowl, or mixing. Older children can measure ingredients, crack eggs, or cut things into pieces using a plastic knife. Always supervise a child around any kind of knife.

◆ Let children taste the different ingredients as you put them into the recipe. Encourage them to describe the taste and texture. Is it *sweet? Dry? Sour? Chewy?* Remember to never let children try raw egg, fish, poultry, or meat.

◆ Look through cookbooks with your child and let her help you plan some meals or snacks for the week. Try to help her choose simple recipes that you can prepare together.

Kids Can Help!

It's never too early to cook with your child. Kids of every age can help in the kitchen and all the recipes in this book are great for preparing together. We've given some suggestions and hints on how kids can be involved with each one of them. So, get ready to start cooking!

Zoe's Tutu Pink Smoothies

Let kids peel the bananas, then break or cut them into chunks with a plastic knife to put in the blender. They can also help measure the yogurt and milk. Let children make the fruit kabobs, but supervise them around the bamboo skewers. Drinking straws can be used instead of skewers, but kids may need help getting the fruit on. Perhaps they could make fruit patterns on a flat surface before the adult puts the fruit on skewers.

Cookie Monster's Monster Muffin Pizzas

Kids will get a kick out of making their own pizzas. Allow them to spoon the sauce on each muffin, sprinkle the cheese on top, and make their own designs with the toppings. Can they make a face like Elmo did? Never leave children around a hot oven unattended. When shopping for the toppings, encourage kids to pick their own colorful array of healthy vegetable toppings.

Big Bird's Peanut Butter Eggs

Kids can crush the graham crackers. Put the crackers in a Ziploc bag and ask them to crunch them up with their hands. Kids can help mix, but the dough may be too stiff for younger children. When shaping the eggs, put a little non-stick spray or flour on kids' hands so the dough doesn't stick.

Ernie's Tasty Twiddlebug Logs and Bert's Boats

Ask kids to wash and dry the celery stalks. Put the cream cheese and/or peanut butter in an easy-to-access container for easier scooping. It may be easier to use a spoon instead of a plastic knife to stuff the stalks. Supervise children when they are making the sails for Bert's Boats with the toothpicks.

Grover's ABC Sandwiches

Put out all the prepared ingredients and let your child assemble his own sandwich. As he assembles the sandwich, name the first letter of each ingredient and the name of the food. Can he make a sandwich using things that start with letters from his name or initials?

Oscar's Delicious Cups of Dirt

Kids can help with every step of this fun recipe—from dumping the milk and pudding mix into the bowl, to crushing the chocolate graham crackers in a Ziploc bag, to spooning the mixture into cups and adding the gummy worms.

Rosita's Cream Cheese Salsa Pinwheels

Children can mix the salsa and cream cheese with a wooden spoon. They will also enjoy spreading the mixture on the tortilla. With assistance, older children can roll them and help wrap them in plastic wrap.

Elmo's Favorite Goldfish Snack Mix

Shake! Shake! Shake! is the fun part of this recipe. After helping to measure all the ingredients and putting each in its own bowl, kids will get a kick out of shaking them all up to mix.

Eat Your Colors Every Day to Keep Your Body Healthy and Fit!

WHITE

GREEN

YELLOW/ORANGE

BLUE/PURPLE

RED

To learn more, go to www.5aday.org

Strawberries, celery, broccoli, and apples… These are just some of the colorful fruits and vegetables kids will find in the recipes of this book. They will help your child get the recommended five or more servings of fruits and vegetables each day. Teaching children to "eat their colors" is a great, fun way to encourage healthy eating from a very young age.

Review the food color wheel above with your child and ask him to name other fruits and vegetables that he can think of for each color. Try to make a "rainbow salad" using one fruit or vegetable of each color (ie: tomato, carrot, corn niblets, lettuce, purple cabbage, and cauliflower).

Here are some other ways to make fruits and veggies a favorite with your child:

◆ Keep lots of fruits and vegetables accessible to your child. Convenient snacks are more likely to be chosen this way.

◆ If possible, plant a couple of vegetable plants in the garden for children to care for. Not only is this a good way to show kids that vegetables don't grow in supermarkets, but they will be more likely to try something they've helped grow. Zucchini, grape tomatoes, and bell peppers are good choices.

◆ Play a guessing game by blindfolding your child and offering her different things to try. Is the food *sweet* or *salty*? *Crunchy* or *creamy*? *Cold* or *warm*? By the time the game is over, she'll have eaten a serving of healthy food! Now it's your turn to try the foods.

◆ Kids are more apt to eat raw vegetables when they can dip them. Mix these ingredients together for a tasty, healthy vegetable dip: 8 ounces of low-fat cream cheese and 8 ounces of low-fat French salad dressing.